THIS BOOK BELONGS TO

The lyrics to the song "Santa Mouse" (© 1966 Michael Martin Brown)
are used with the permission of Brownstone Music, Inc.

LITTLE SIMON
An imprint of Simon & Schuster Children's Publishing Division
1230 Avenue of the Americas, New York, New York 10020
This Little Simon hardcover edition September 2019
Copyright © 1966 by Michael Martin Brown; copyright renewed © 1994 by Michael Martin Brown
Originally published by Grosset & Dunlap.
All rights reserved, including the right of reproduction in whole or in part in any form.
LITTLE SIMON is a registered trademark of Simon & Schuster, Inc., and associated colophon is a trademark of
Simon & Schuster, Inc. For information about special
discounts for bulk purchases, please contact Simon & Schuster Special Sales
at 1-866-506-1949 or business@simonandschuster.com.
The Simon & Schuster Speakers Bureau can bring authors to your live event.
For more information or to book an event contact the Simon & Schuster Speakers Bureau
at 1-866-248-3049 or visit our website at www.simonspeakers.com.
Design and title lettering by Angela Navarra
Manufactured in China 0719 SCP
2 4 6 8 10 9 7 5 3 1
Full CIP data for this book is available from the Library of Congress.
ISBN 978-1-5344-3793-7 (hc)
ISBN 978-1-5344-3794-4 (eBook)

SANTA MOUSE

by MICHAEL BROWN
illustrated by ELFRIEDA DE WITT

LITTLE SIMON

New York London Toronto Sydney New Delhi

Once there was a little mouse
who didn't have a name.

He lived in a great big house,
this mouse,
the only mouse in the whole,
wide house.

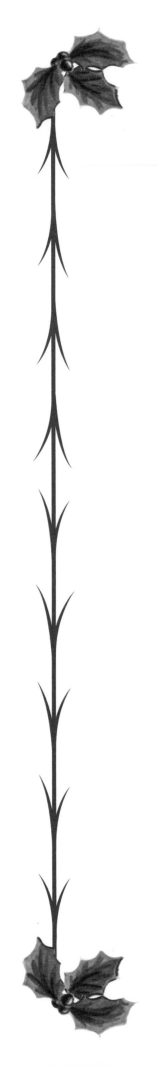

He used to play a game.
He'd daydream he had playmates
who were friendly as could be.

While some of them
would bring their dolls
and dress up and have tea,

there were
others who'd

play cowboys,

or be Inuit,

or Spanish.

But when he tried to touch them,

like a bubble
they would vanish.

Now, through the year,
this little mouse
had saved one special thing:

a piece of cheese!

The kind that makes an
ANGEL WANT TO SING.

ON CHRISTMAS EVE,

he brushed his teeth,

and as he washed his paws,

he thought,
"My goodness, no one gives
A GIFT TO SANTA CLAUS!"

He ran to get his
pretty cheese,
and after he had found it,

the paper from some chewing gum
he quickly wrapped around it.

And then he climbed in bed and dreamed

that he was
lifted high.

He woke to find that he was
looking right in Santa's eye!

"I thank you for my gift,"
said Santa.

"Tell me, what's your name?"

"I haven't any," said the mouse.

"You haven't? That's a shame!"

"You know, I need a helper
as I travel house to house,
and I shall give a name to you.

I'll call you
SANTA
MOUSE."

"So here's your beard,

and here's your suit,

and here's each shiny,

tiny

boot."

"You mustn't sneeze,
and don't you cough.

Just put them on,
and we'll be off!"

Then over all the rooftops,
on a journey with no end,
away they went together,
Santa with his tiny friend.

And so, this Christmas,
if you please, beneath the
tree that's in your house,

why don't you leave
a piece of cheese?

You know who'll thank you?

Santa
Mouse!

THE
SANTA MOUSE SONG
words and music by Michael Brown

Who's the little friend
on Santa's shoulder?
Santa Mouse!

Who is it we look
for when it's colder?
Santa Mouse!

He's the one who once was just
a mouse without a name
till he did a deed so very kind
when Christmas came.

Oh, who's the one who
thought about a gift for
Santa Claus?

Who's the one who wrapped
a piece of cheese up
with his paws?

Who's the little fellow with the
biggest heart in all the house
and with the whiskers?

Is it any wonder Santa named him
Santa Mouse?

THE END